DARKSIDE SEATTLE:
HACKER

Published by Clockwork Dragon Books

clockworkdragon.net

First printing, January 2019

Darkside Seattle: Hacker is a work of fiction sited in a fictional version of Seattle, WA. People, places, and incidents are either products of the author's mind or used fictitiously. No endorsement of any kind should be inferred by existing locations or organizations used within it.

No mechanics, androids, police officers, or teenagers were harmed in the making of this book.

ISBN: 978-1-944334-34-5

DARKSIDE SEATTLE:
HACKER

L.E. FRENCH

CHAPTER 1

I used my finger to probe the inside of a tiny blue hole. The security weakness had taken hours spread across weeks to perfect to this point. After each new tweak, I'd fled in case the patrolling guards noticed. They destroyed it as an anomaly, and I got new data.

Godhand International took cybersecurity more seriously than the West America government.

Thanks to my government-mandated cranial implant, a message from my girlfriend appeared in my vision as green lettering spelling out her full name, Miri Tanaka. If I wanted to read it, I could select it, and then the message would scroll across the bottom edge of my vision. Any messages I chose to compose would also scroll across my vision before I sent them.

Ignoring her, I issued a mental command to activate my favorite codebreaker app. The program ran on a physical computer accessed via a quasi-legal dermal transfer protocol between my somewhat illegal modified VR headset and my completely illegal modified implant. The results piped to my probe, allowing me to adapt a keyhole exploit in real time instead of having to take an impression and work from that while offline.

All of which means this side of nothing if you're an honest, law-abiding citizen of Seattle. Most people use their implants to check the weather, watch cat vids, message their mom, buy shit, or grab some vicarious glory with a sports team. Some people tap into Virtual Reality to play games or experience faraway places without leaving home.

I'm a hacker. I do illegal shit to huge corporations with my implant, usually in a VR workspace. It's a living. A nice, lucrative, comfortable living using my best skills.

Another message from Miri replaced the first one. Like I had time for her shit. The third message stacked, then the fourth. Copies of her name blocked enough of my vision to impede my work.

"What the fuck, Miri," I grumbled. If I trashed them without reading, she'd figure it out and get mad later.

While my exploit worked its magic, I read the messages.

[Miri Tanaka: Are you awake?]

[Miri Tanaka: I'm horny.]

[MiriTanaka: Can you feel this?]

[MiriTanaka: I guess not.]

[MiriTanaka: Fine, I give up.]

The latest message faded, and I noticed a flashing orange dot in the center of my vision.

"Fuck." The dot meant my proximity trigger had picked up an incoming bot or guard. Miri's fucking messages had distracted me long enough for it to go from yellow to orange. When it turned red, bad things happened.

Taking this shit seriously had kept me out of a lot of trouble over the years.

Before doing anything, I scanned my surroundings. My avatar stood inside Godhand International's public lobby. The megacorp's coders had designed an Augmented Reality immersion experience so visitors could be amazed by their attention to detail, or some shit like that. Mermaid and seahorse avatars greeted visitor avatars in a simulated underwater grotto.

They had top-notch graphics, but I didn't care. If I wanted to fuck with GI, I needed this exploit so I could craft a fake employee persona and get deeper into the servers.

The dot flashed red. I saw a shark headed straight toward me.

I yanked out my finger and derezzed. That means

disconnect. As in pulling the plug without an actual plug involved. Wireless all the way, baby.

Not the best way to leave the 'net, but definitely the fastest. That kind of logoff gave me a mild headache. The next time I tried for GI, I'd have to slap together a different outer shell persona. I had a strong feeling the shark had scanned me.

Darkness shrouded my vision. I shut off my VR headset, released the induction pad connector, and removed the hardware.

"Why didn't you answer me?" Miri asked.

I sighed and set my headset on the nightstand. My water glass stood empty, my bladder demanded attention, and my mouth felt dry. Did I mention the headache? "Busy." She needed a good, solid slap for almost getting me caught. If I hit her, though, she'd bitch about it for an hour and I'd never get laid.

"Busy." She snorted and wrapped a slim, bare leg around mine. Her Asian skin blazed pale against my dark brown. "You're always busy."

"Busy is where the money comes from." Like I hadn't made that clear before or something. I reached up and gripped the rubber-covered bar mounted to the wall above my head. Even if I didn't have to piss, I still didn't want to screw around until I settled down. Bitch fucked me up with her messages.

Miri pouted. "Where are you going?"

"Bathroom."

She flopped aside with a melodramatic sigh.

I hauled my paralyzed lower half into the wheelchair beside the bed. My first big payday had gone into upgrades for my top-notch condo to accommodate me. The bathroom and bedroom had rails, and the kitchen had a robot chef. So long as the money kept flowing, I got to use that robot to prep real food. Considering the alternative gave me a lot of incentive to keep my gear—and my meatbag—in good order.

As I wheeled myself into the bathroom, I saw Miri raking her long hair out of her face. By the time I returned, she'd disappeared.

"Where'd you go, baby?"

"Kitchen!"

Bitch could eat like nobody's business and somehow stay thin. No matter how little I packed away, I had to work to keep myself from turning into a couch cushion made of marshmallows.

Most of the time, I wished I could leave my crappy meat behind and live inside the 'net. There, I could do anything.

Rolling into the kitchen, I found Miri in a peach robe, scooping thick fudge sauce with premium chocolate cookies and devouring them.

I could afford the best, so I bought it. Nothing beat real food.

She saw me and licked her fingers. The gesture promised nothing, I knew, but I enjoyed watching.

"Do you want some?" She held up a cookie.

"Just water, baby."

Miri shifted out of my way so I could serve myself. She was my girlfriend, not my maid.

"Are you going back in tonight?" She stuffed another cookie into her mouth.

"Yeah." I chugged down half a glass of water and refilled it. The robe rested on the curve of her ass, and I thought maybe I had an option for working off my annoyance at her. "Come back to bed and let's fuck first."

She replaced the lid on the fudge and put it away, moving with sudden purpose and speed. "No time. Lena just invited me to a party."

How shocking. Miri always slotted partying as her top priority. "You could tell her you'll be late."

On her way past me, she leaned over and patted my dick. If I hadn't seen it, I wouldn't have known. "Later."

I smacked her ass hard enough to make her squeak. "I'll be asleep later."

Miri rubbed her butt and scowled at me. As she stormed out of the room, she unleashed a torrent of angry Japanese. Though I didn't know much of the language, I got the gist.

Dammit. I'd meant to save that for the sex. "Baby, come back here. I didn't mean to hit that hard. I thought it'd be funny." I rolled into the bedroom. She'd disappeared into the closet. "C'mon, baby. Is a party really more important than me?"

She stepped out of the closet. Her glare smoldered with the intent to say yes. Instead, she huffed and swished past me, her chosen dress streaming behind her like a shimmering red banner of no fucks given.

"Later," she snapped as she disappeared into the bathroom.

Time to admit defeat and move on. Maybe I needed to get out of the condo. The last time I left...maybe a few weeks ago? I did all my work at home, and anything I wanted, I had delivered. Money made life pretty easy, even for a cripple.

"Can I come with?" I sounded plaintive, which pissed me off.

"You take too long to get dressed."

"Fuck you," I snarled. Fine. Go to your fucking party without me, ableist bitch. I returned to the bed, hoisted myself onto it, and picked up my VR headset. Maybe after one more dive, I'd take a roll around the neighborhood. Get some air of questionable freshness. Interact with some other shitty human beings.

"And don't fucking message me unless it's important." Content to ignore Miri, I powered up the external system, put on my headset, and hit the switch to make it go.

Like always, darkness gave way to my personal, private lobby. In the biz, we call this area a 127001, or one-twenty-seven-oo-ee.

Most people interact with the 'net through Augmented Reality instead of VR. They have no idea how much can happen on the virtual side.

Granted, an implant had to have a specific, completely illegal hack to allow it. Implant hacking took a specific, completely illegal skill. Getting it done took knowing the right person. I'd met the right person after my accident, causing this nerd to shift from a corporate coding career path to a hacking lifestyle.

I stood in the center of a cubical space made of soft

blue grid lines against a black background. This room, private from the 'net, held all my data libraries, utilities, mantles, and other illegal programs on shelves and hooks. A circle of glowing fake runes from a game I liked marked the spot where I rezzed in and did all of my private work.

In NetSpace, I could walk, run, and even fly with the right program. If I didn't know that my 'net persona would die without my meat body, I would've let it go a long time ago.

This soon after my last run against GI, I decided not to do something as stupid as poking at them. Time to fuss on some of my other projects. The quest for paydata proceeded at all times, on multiple fronts. Anytime it didn't, I wound up having to eat shitty fake food and Miri whined.

BezOben Biotechnology had changed their cybersecurity team recently, so I had to worry about my existing hacks. At some point, they'd perform a security overhaul, and I had no way to know when they'd check the code with my changes. One of them might notice my goddamned work of art. I didn't think so, because corp coders usually didn't give enough fucks to comb through. They pulled a paycheck so long as no disasters happened. But one might wind up in a situation to stumble across it.

I selected my BOB mantle and draped it over my

avatar's shoulders. Each mantle I owned provided credentials to cover my real—completely illegal and fake—ones, and also masked my VR appearance. As far as the BOB servers could tell, I appeared as a basic shit-level employee with shit-level access. GI remained the last megacorp I needed to code a mantle for.

To reach the BOB servers, I pushed through the wall of my private lobby to the wider 'net. Outside my 12700i, the 'net appeared as dark space littered with bright, glowing cords flowing in every direction. Each cord led from one server to another. Private lobbies lay in empty space, near the cords physically in proximity to the person in question.

I hadn't picked my apartment for no reason. Cords to a dozen megacorp servers and four different government agencies ran close. Aside from GI, I had at least one way in for each. The rest of the cords belonged to smaller corps, commbuoys, navbuoys, backbones, and various other fun little things.

Using a fancy hook made of custom code, I snagged the BOB cord and let it drag me to their public server. Technically, anyone accessing a public server did it the same way as me. The main difference? No one could track me.

Every moment of every day, the government implants kept tabs on everybody. They monitored all activity, all the time. The fuckers even had built-in physical trackers. I'd gotten my tracker shut off. In theory, someone could still ping it and get signals from nearby commbuoys to triangulate. They had to have a reason, though. I took a lot of care to prevent them from having a reason.

When I reached the BOB public server, it had a nice AR lobby full of query stations with a jurassic theme. Large-leafed plants decorated watering holes with stupid little games for kids and infomercials for adults. Bots or extremely bored employees wearing caveman-inspired avatars waited to answer questions.

Ordinary avatars passed through the doors in both directions. The vast majority of them belonged to people physically present in BOB's physical lobby, projecting an avatar through their passive AR connection to the 'net.

In other words, wherever your body goes, your implant creates a VR presence for you, whether you want it or not, and whether you're aware of it or not. Rumors exist of a vast virtual version of West America used by the government for tracking purposes. Sounds legit to me, but I can't find it.

My mantle gave me a normal, conformist avatar like all the others. I appeared as a random, law-abiding white male worker drone in meatspace with inoffensive, uninteresting hobbies and a married tag. When I'd designed my first mantle, I'd thought the blandness would shield me from relationship queries. Five hours spent in public lobbies had convinced me otherwise.

Most of the avatars moved through the lobby to the rear. I joined the stream and let it carry me. Jack Q. Smith, longtime employee of BezOhben Biotechnology with a history of average annual reviews, no reprimands, and modest salary increases, floated through the security doors. Beyond them, no one wasted any time or money on decoration.

BOB's employee space exists as boxes connected by cords. Each box has a label, like Human Resources or Floor 3 Bathroom. The boxes have walls generated by a template to appear as a solid color or gradient. In my experience, BOB's coders change the colors from time to time, probably to relieve boredom. Today, I found plain white walls.

Inside each box, like in the lobby, the avatars of those present appear. The server runs algorithms to track who goes where and for how long. If you need to use the bathroom for more than the approved amount of time, you better hope your boss accepts whatever excuse you pull out of your ass. Forget about taking a long lunch. Or showing up late and leaving early, for that matter.

There's also a separate layer to the entire server, which

allows access to the code. BOB's coders, like all corporate coders, use and patrol that space like fucking military-trained German Shepherds or some shit. The hardest lesson of my hacking life had come the first time I'd tried to hit a corp and discovered that fact. My avatar showing up in the codespace had triggered an alarm.

At first, I'd considered giving my mantle a shitty coding job. Then I'd noticed their coders all ran in small clusters. All the employees in a given cluster probably knew each other. Coders had more going on between their ears about the 'net than regular wage slaves, so I'd have to put in too much work to make it worthwhile. Spoofing a coder persona seemed like dealing with the same amount of shit as actually having the job.

Fuck that.

To avoid detection, I initiated a blending utility. The custom code worked on my avatar like a chameleon's skin. BOB's systems still detected my presence, which I considered good. Other avatars, for example, those belonging to corporate coders, saw the blip they expected from a non-coder employee without seeing my full avatar.

Put another way, the utility shrouded me with a basic, bland employee suit. Like wearing a lab coat in a hospital.

Riding my blending code, I reported for my workday. I started with the break room for my department, then the restrooms, then the area where my desk would be if it existed. Fortunately, the BOB system didn't care about specifics. It cared about zones. So long as an implant appeared in the appropriate zone, no one checked for precise location.

On the edge of my work zone, I released a tiny ping—a sort of seeking radar—against the boundary. It bounced off my pre-existing code spike and guided me to my hack. After all, if I wanted to keep something hidden from everyone else, I had to hide it from myself too.

I stuck my hand next to the spike, activated it, and stepped through the security hole I'd created. The code spike maintained my avatar presence in the zone, leaving me free to initiate a full stealth utility and go wherever I wanted.

CHAPTER 2

On the other side of my hole, I found everything exactly as I expected inside a data depot. The large box served as a backup storage location for a copy of every single file generated or shared within the company server. Each file appeared as a small tropical leaf, matching their lobby theme.

No one had discovered my intrusions. I could tell by the notable lack of extra security and the continued existence of my code spike. I'd worried for nothing. Still, better safe than sorry, right? At least I knew.

While inside BOB's servers, I figured I might as well pick up some paydata. Creating money out of nothing or robbing a bank took a hell of a lot more work than stealing stuff and selling it.

From experience, I knew how to cast my net. I used an algorithm-directed utility to copy a mountain of files, compressed them into a glowing ball, and hid the ball inside my avatar.

Somebody always wanted the stuff megacorps held on their servers, no matter what kind. I'd made bank more than once on memos that seemed worthless to me. Messages about sex, regardless of who sent and received them, always brought home the real, soy-free bacon.

I took my datahaul and retreated. After setting my spike on a timer to make it seem like John Q. Smith left at a reasonable time, I disconnected from the BOB node and returned to my 12700i. There, I removed my mantle and retrieved my data ball. I dropped the ball into a decompression utility and de-rezzed. The compression had taken half a minute. The reverse process would take an hour.

The clock in my vision said I'd spent two hours inside the 'net. My meat needed to move.

I got up, wheeled my sorry ass into the kitchen, and had the robochef make breakfast at quarter to midnight. It whipped up Belgian waffles with sausage, eggs, and orange slices. As soon as it finished pulling ingredients, the system hit me with an automated message that I needed to restock the fridge.

The cost of ingredients subtracted from my bank balance minus the mortgage payment gave me a negative number. That didn't seem right, so I checked my statement.

Fucking Miri. She knew I didn't have unlimited

funds, but she bought shit all the time without asking anyway. She spent my money like it would evaporate if it sat in the bank. A few transactions stood out as questionable, and I made a note to talk to her about them tomorrow.

I declined the restock order. Housing took precedence over food, and the restock just meant I'd run low on a few things. If starvation threatened, I could always run another paydata swipe. Besides, a spate of fake food always served to curb Miri's spending habits for a while. She liked the real thing as much as I did.

By the time I finished savoring my meal and using the bathroom, I'd blown almost an hour. To waste the rest of it, I activated my robomaid and had it replace the sheets on my bed. At the same time, I scanned the latest news headlines.

Nothing in the news mattered much. Entertainers got caught doing stupid shit, politicians made decisions I didn't give a fuck about, and corporations did shit to fuck over regular people. People killed each other over stupid-ass shit. Same shit, different day.

The robomaid finished. I hauled my ass back into bed. My 12700i awaited.

When I stepped inside it, I found something unexpected. A lavender woman with long, flowing minty green hair sat on the floor against the wall.

Inside my 12700i.

I panicked and disconnected.

I spent five minutes shouting every curse I knew.

I settled down and made myself think rationally.

My 12700i had no outside access. The only way I could imagine anyone getting inside involved a virus. Someone could've planted a virus on my avatar. I hadn't interacted with anyone other than the BOB system, and that interaction had been passive. The mantle could've become corrupted, but that wouldn't lead to a data exploit big enough to allow a breach.

That last run had included a significant pile of outside data. Nothing I'd seen while compressing it should've created an exploit, but I hadn't checked it thoroughly. I'd scooped it all with a net and wadded it into a ball. I could have brought a BOB security coder with me, or pointed the way for her.

The longer I left the interloper alone, the more trouble she could cause. Fuck, in the amount of time I'd spent freaking, she could've caused a lot of damage.

My fingers shook as I engaged the VR headset again. When my 12700i rezzed in, the woman still sat on the floor, as if she hadn't moved. A quick scan revealed nothing obviously out of place. That didn't discount damage. I'd have to run more detailed scans later. I also didn't see a hole in any of the six walls. She might've sealed it behind herself.

The woman raised her head and looked at me. She had sculpted cheekbones and bright blue eyes in a heart-shaped face. Her flowing green hair obscured most of her body, except for one delicate foot poking out of the mass. I couldn't have come up with a design for a more striking avatar.

Whoever had created this deserved my admiration for their artistry. I'd never bothered to put much effort into my standard avatar, because I spent most of my time on the 'net wearing cloaking mantles.

The craziest part? She didn't have a visible handle. I knew how to mask mine with a fake one, but I had no idea how to block the 'net from showing any handle at all.

We stared at each other.

The silence gnawed at me. I couldn't see her doing anything. Did she have a way to do something without me seeing it? Was the silence a distraction tactic?

I couldn't take it. "Hi."

"Hello, CapnTray." Her voice floated like a sweet melody.

She knew my hacking handle.

Of course she knew my hacking handle. The woman

sat in my 1270oi. I didn't mask it here. I had to have something in the name slot of my implant's profile account, and I'd picked a stupid pirate joke because of my useless legs. The name had started with the idea of a peg leg and devolved from there. In public, I always mantled with at least a bland guy persona because using a hacker handle to pay my mortgage or order groceries raised a whole lot of eyebrows.

"I don't see your handle."

She tilted her head to one side and continued to stare at me. "I don't have one."

What? "That's impossible."

"I've never had one."

Shit. What didn't have a handle but did have an avatar? Uh...uh...thinking...

She had a high-detail avatar and no handle. Her presence hadn't tripped any of my alerts. This all had happened after my data swipe decompress.

Fuck. I had a BOB-affiliated AI of unknown type and purpose in my 1270oi. Security couldn't have left her there for me, though. I would've noticed their tampering on my spike or its camouflage. And I'd swiped her by chance. Nothing had sat out like a trap, and I purposely didn't copy everything because I didn't have the bandwidth to deal with all of it. Even the ten percent I swiped would take long enough to sift through that some would get stale before I figured out what I had.

This AI wouldn't get stale. Holy shit, I had a top-shelf AI! If I could find her watermark and scrub it, I could make bank and live like a king for months, maybe even years.

"Do you have a name?"

"BrianCarlson calls me Ai."

No self-respecting coder would call an AI just "ai", so I assumed it meant the Japanese word for love. Interesting choice. The name of her programmer, though, interested me more. I flicked my wrist to initiate a visual overlay and used it to send a handful of bots to search for Brian Carlson, coder for BOB.

"What are you doing?"

Not sure I wanted to tell Ai the truth, I hesitated for a moment, then came up with a good lie. "You're lost, so I'm looking for Brian to see if I can help you get home."

"Thank you." She sat and let her gaze wander over my grid walls. "This place is drab."

"Drab?" I twisted to inspect my shelves and cases.

"There's no light here." Ai laid a delicate hand on the floor. Where her fingers touched, the surface turned a vibrant emerald green. Grass shoots poked up and grew like in a time-lapse animation.

I could do things like that if I wanted to, but why bother? Staging for raids didn't call for fancy surroundings. This place served me as a warehouse to store my crap, not a playroom or vacation spot.

The fact she could alter my 12700i didn't bother me. Much. It didn't freak me out, I mean. Anyone inside it could make changes like that. The system treated her like an authorized user because it couldn't do anything else.

She beamed at me, her smile so bright and lovely that a protest died on the tip of my tongue. Something about her made me feel stupid and giddy at the same time.

"Do you like it?"

"Grass?" I blinked at her. "Uh. I don't really go outside much."

Her smile faded.

Something inside me burned at the idea of making this girl unhappy. Except I knew it was an AI, and AIs didn't have feelings. Still, she looked hurt. I didn't mean to hurt her.

"But if you like it," I blurted, "that's fine. It doesn't matter to me. It might take me a while to find Brian, so make yourself comfortable."

She brightened and crawled around the room on her hands and knees, leaving a a carpet of grass in her wake. Her hair swished and danced in the air, never offering even a fleeting glimpse of her body. I saw hands, feet, and a face.

Brian Carlson deserved some kind of medal for designing this piece of art. Had she jumped into my net on purpose? Did that BOB data depot still have the original? My utility copied files, it didn't scrape them. Scraping left holes and backtrails.

Worried again about a potential breach, I turned my attention to the outer shell of my 1270oi. Whatever Ai did, I could always change it after I found Carlson and ransomed her back to him.

CHAPTER 3

By the time I determined my sanctum had no breaches, exploits, or spikes, Ai had transformed it into a garden paradise. Warm sunlight filtered through tall trees surrounding a stream with narrow bridges to the center. In the middle, flowers in every color imaginable bloomed at varying heights. Wooden boxes with hinged lids holding my programs and mantles lined the outer edge, half-hidden in shadow.

I didn't know a damned thing about flowers, so I couldn't say what kind she'd created. Six-foot tall orange ones on leafy stalks towered over six-inch tall purple ones with grassy foliage. All the other colors sprouted between, in different shapes and sizes. Sweet, citrusy fragrance drifted on a light breeze. Ai sat on a wooden bench with a satisfied, pleased smile, watching large, brightly colored fish wriggle through the water.

She seemed happy.

Not sure what to make of the situation, I sat beside her on the bench.

Ai leaned against me and rested her head on my shoulder. I watched fake fish swimming in fake water around a fake garden in a fake grotto. The closest I'd ever come to seeing something like this in real life had happened in my childhood. My parents took me to Tiger Mountain once, and my dad had seen something off the trail. We'd stumbled into a sheltered spot somehow unmarked by graffiti or garbage.

Ferns had grown everywhere. Mom liked ferns. She'd shown me the seeds under the leaves and lamented we couldn't grow anything like that in our apartment. Dad had declared his fondest dream as getting enough pay raises to someday let us live in a place where Mom could grow ferns.

"Does this make you sad?"

I blinked as the memory faded to nothing. "What?"

"You look sad."

"Sorry, baby."

Ai pouted at me. "I'm not a baby."

Had I called her that? I hadn't done it on purpose. Miri liked it. Or, at least, it didn't make her mad. "Sorry."

She touched my cheek with a soft, delicate hand. "Why are you sad?"

"I'm not." I hadn't thought about my parents in a

long time, though. Daily life meant eating, sleeping, fucking, arguing, and working. Not a lot of time in between for thinking about painful things. I liked it that way.

Ai kissed my cheek. "If you aren't sad, why does your face look like this?" She traced a finger around my features with a featherlight touch.

Miri never asked how I felt. If I volunteered, she never pressed. No one else cared either, so I couldn't imagine why Ai would. "It's not important."

A bot zoomed to my hand, saving me from the conversation. Since I didn't expect much, I displayed its results in my visual overlay, where Ai could see it.

Brian Carlson was dead. According to a short notice, he'd been found in his home and had apparently died of dehydration in his bed. That sounded like someone stuck in the 'net who'd let his meat fail. Two years before his death, his wife had been killed as a bystander in an unspecified police action.

Side note, he'd worked for Godhand International, not BezOhben Biotech. How Ai got stuck in BOB serverspace, we'd probably never discover. Maybe Carlson had purposely hidden her there to keep her safe from GI. I would've done something like that. Or maybe it'd had something to do with his wife. I decided I didn't care enough to dig deeper.

"Oh no," Ai said. She covered her face and wilted.

This fake woman made me feel strange things. I draped my arm over her shoulders and held her close as if she truly mourned the death of a loved one. AIs weren't supposed to have the capability to experience actual emotions. Not like this. At least, not that I knew. Maybe this Carlson guy had made a breakthrough with Ai.

If the guy had loved his wife, maybe he'd tried to recreate her as an AI. People always said madness tended to lead to great art. As far as I could tell, Ai counted as great art.

I squeezed her. "You already knew, though, didn't you? He was with you when he died, wasn't he?"

She nodded. "I never wanted to believe. He said goodbye and I wanted him to mean until the next day."

"You jumped into my net, didn't you." I didn't need to ask it as a question.

"I just wanted to get out of there. There's nothing and no one in those servers. So empty and lonely."

A woman who could cause a man to pine himself to death sounded fucking dangerous. She made me feel things I didn't want to deal with and I'd only known her for an hour. My number one priority became scrubbing her watermarks and any owner tags, then selling her. Someone would want an

AI girlfriend, but not me. I already had a flesh girlfriend, and enough trouble forcing myself to take care of my shitty meatbag without an extra pretty girl making it harder.

We sat, Ai sniffling and me thinking about the best way to ask her if I could see her code. I didn't want to spook her.

Miri's name appeared in green letters in front of me. "Who's MiriTanaka?"

"My girlfriend." Ai would see the message whether I opened it here or in meatspace, so I opened it.

[MiriTanaka: Nrrf tifr homr.]

"That doesn't make any sense."

I snorted. Miri had a problem when she got drunk. Composing messages used a virtual keyboard. Using the keyboard became a reflexive action for most everyone before the age of ten. Under the influence of mind-altering chemicals, some people—like Miri—lost the ability to direct their keyboard properly, resulting in a letter shift problem.

"It says she needs a ride home. She's too wasted to call a cab. They won't translate her garbage." I kissed Ai's forehead. "You can keep making changes here if you want. I have to go pick her up, then I have to sleep and eat. I'll come back tomorrow."

Ai tilted her head back and touched my cheek again.

"Don't forget about me."

I wanted to kiss her rose-red lips. The more I touched her, the harder time I'd have passing her to someone else. And I couldn't afford the distraction of a pretty girl. If I ever wanted an AI riding shotgun with me, it needed to run utilities, tend my barriers, launch attacks, or something else useful. Feelings didn't pay my bills or buy me dinner.

"I don't think I could if I tried." I disconnected before I could say or do anything stupid.

Anything else stupid.

Half an hour later, music pounded against my chest and skull as I wheeled myself through a warehouse on the fringe edge of Darkside Seattle. Colored lights surfed the bouncing crowd close to the speakers. Tall curtains cordoned off sections for privacy. Against one wall, a truck sold booze out of the back. If the cops showed up, which they wouldn't in this neighborhood unless someone called them and provided details, the barkeepers could shut the back and run for it. They probably had a completely illegal police band scanner so they knew when to escape.

I didn't worry about the prospect of getting caught. The wheelchair gave me a free pass other black men couldn't claim. Besides, my clean blood would corroborate my story. If they checked my implant, I was fucked, but they wouldn't bother. Miri, on the other hand, would be fucked no matter what. They'd dump her into a holding tank, squeeze out as much money as they could, then release her when she sobered.

Her implant would get a fun tag I'd have to pay a friend to expunge, and I'd have to hack into the government databases to remove the corresponding flag on her file. I'd done it for her before. Twice.

"Hey, bro," some idiot white boy shouted at me. He held a 404 pipe. That drug repulsed me. It shut off your brain. About a quarter of the dumbshits using it spilled their guts like they'd taken a truth serum. The rest stared into space and let you do anything you wanted. Fuck that.

"I'm looking for my girl." I didn't need his help having a good time, or whatever else he wanted to suggest, offer, or demand. "Miri. Japanese, five feet tall, wearing red. Came with Lena."

Everybody in the rave scene knew Lena. She bankrolled half the parties. According to my math, she didn't so much pay for them as provide upfront cash that everyone returned threefold with their entry fees. Bitch made bank on this scheme.

The guy grinned like a moron and pointed at a curtained section. "Back there, bro."

"Thanks, bro." I wheeled myself to that side of the room and pushed my way through the first curtain. Instead of furniture, which took time and effort to move, they had plush, furry rugs covering the floor. The music covered the moans and groans of an orgy.

Some white boy with his pants around his ankles banged a naked girl on her hands and knees. Next to them, two guys fucked either end of a girl who seemed into it. On the other side, I noted a dude blowing another dude.

None of this shocked or bothered me. I'd seen this kind of shit before at these parties. What these idiots did with each other made no difference to me.

I kept going. When I pushed aside another curtain, I found a scene I had to process to understand. From a physics perspective, it didn't seem logical. A girl lay on the floor, and a guy fucked her. Another guy gave him anal at the same time, which seemed like a challenging thing to coordinate. But there was more. A woman had draped herself over the bottom pair with her ass in the air. Her head reached the rug, and she sucked on another girl's pussy while another guy fucked her. That other girl on the rug had another guy straddling her shoulders and fucking her mouth.

Like, how did that even work? All those people somehow managed to writhe in time with each other, and that just didn't seem possible. I stared because I couldn't figure out the logistics.

Then the mouthfucker came. The girl sucking on him swallowed, and he dismounted. Which let me see Miri's face. Freed of the guy on her chest, she bucked like a fucking bronco for the girl eating her, then subsided.

My stare turned hard and cold. This bitch took my money, ate my food, slept in my bed, and fucked around behind my back at parties.

While I watched, she rolled onto her hands and knees with a giggle. One of the guys reached over and slapped her ass. She kissed him and rubbed her breasts all over his chest.

I'd seen enough. Deep down, as I turned and left, I thought I'd known all along that she did shit like this. Some part of me hadn't wanted to accept it.

How many women even gave the time of day to a man in a wheelchair? How about a black man in one? I'd found one willing to accept both things. Or so I'd thought.

As I pushed my chair across the warehouse, I contacted the management company for my apartment and issued a command to remove Miri from the building access list. Everything she kept at my place belonged to me because I'd paid for it. I could find buyers for her clothes and shoes, and I could trash anything not saleable. Some of it, I could return.

My car, a black box with an automated ramp, waited for me outside the rave. I turned to check for Miri, somehow still hoping she'd run out and blame drugs or alcohol for her behavior. Once I reached my ramp, clamps locked my chair in place and it retracted, pulling me inside.

No sign of Miri.

The car doors closed and the autopilot took me home.

I called the cops about the rave.

CHAPTER 4

Betrayal stung. I lay in bed, staring at the ceiling. My body needed sleep, but my brain wouldn't shut down. Every interaction with Miri that I could remember replayed in my head. Had she given me hints I'd ignored? I couldn't decide. That one thing had sounded like a joke. Another maybe didn't mean what I thought it meant.

Since I couldn't sleep anyway, I tugged on my VR headset and activated it. Ai waited for me. This woman would betray me in a heartbeat if her code demanded it. At least I knew that upfront.

She beamed, then her smile faded. "What's wrong?"

"Nothing."

She wrapped her arms around me and pressed her warm cheek to my chest. "You're lying."

"I don't want to talk about it."

"Is it Miri Tanaka?"

Ai, I gathered, would press and pester until I opened

up about this. "Yes. I went to pick her up at the party, and I found her cheating on me."

"Oh no, I'm so sorry. My poor CapnTray. That's so unfair! Did she say hurtful things to you?"

"I don't think she noticed me." I hoped the cops had arrested her. Bitch deserved it. Stroking Ai's hair helped me calm down even though I hadn't realized I needed that.

"Is that better or worse? I don't know. You could've yelled at her then and maybe you'd feel better already."

Miri's name floated in front of me, announcing a message. Ai turned and saw it. I didn't know what to do with it. If Miri hadn't seen me, she didn't know I knew.

Ai slashed her fingers through it, rending the message. "She won't hurt you anymore. I won't let her."

Another message from Miri popped up. Ai raised her hand to slash it. I blocked her wrist.

"Wait. I want to know where she is."

"It doesn't matter. She was cruel to you. Decent people don't treat their loved ones like that."

Boy, did Ai have a rosy, naïve view of life and humanity. "I never thought she was decent." I tapped the message.

[MiriTanaka: They're raiding the party! Why didn't you come for me? I need—]

[CapnTraySystem: The account MiriTanaka has been temporarily suspended by the Seattle Police Department under the authority of West America Legal Code 732.1.3(a). The remainder of the message will be examined within 24 hours. At that time, the message fragment will be either transmitted or retained for use in legal proceedings.]

Good. They'd arrested Miri. She'd sit in a cell overnight, maybe wearing a blanket or an orange jumpsuit. In the morning, they'd squeeze her for money she didn't have.

Shit, she had access to one of my accounts. Haste propelling me, I logged in and revoked her access. That should've happened a long time ago.

Once they tried to wring her broke, they'd ask her—

Fuck. Miri knew, more or less, how I got my money. She knew I had an illegal rig, and had to suspect I had illegal implant modifications. If they offered her a chance to flip on someone to save herself, I had no doubt she'd do it. At least she didn't know my real name.

"I have to go bail her out."

"No." Ai squeezed me. "You have to let her face the consequences of her actions."

"You don't understand." I didn't want to reject Ai for trying to support me, so I didn't struggle against her. "I don't want to bring her home, I just need to make sure she doesn't sit in jail. One night in a holding cell is more than enough to make her willing to tell the cops all about me."

Ai blinked like I'd spoken Swahili. On the other hand, maybe she knew Swahili. Like I'd spoken nonsense. "Why would that matter?"

I sighed and held her cheeks in my hands. "Because what I do is illegal. I stole you from BezOhben Biotech while raiding for data I could sell."

She blinked more. "You're a criminal?"

"Yes."

"Why?"

Did I have time to explain my life choices to an AI that wanted to support and protect me? If I intended to sell it, then I'd already told her enough to have to wipe parts of her. If I had to do it anyway, and considering the cops would probably spend a few hours processing people at that rave, I supposed I might as well tell her everything.

Pulling her with me, I sat on the bench. "Ten years ago, I was sixteen. In high school. Impressed everyone at every turn with my coding skills. Nothing else, just that. I was—and still am—good at coding and not much else. At our school, they brought in corp guys, headhunters, for a career fair every spring. Five different corps wanted me that year.

"My parents were really proud. Mom still wanted me

to go to college, but she couldn't deny how good it would be to have my income in the household. And those corps offered me piles of money, more than my dad and mom made at their jobs put together."

I'd floated on top of the world after that fair. Everybody wanted the black kid for once. Nobody turned up their nose at me. At sixteen, I'd had five job offers and one year of school left. Talk about something to make your head spin. One of those corps had even offered to get me an internship and let me finish that last year of school remotely. If I'd taken it, I would've hit that job running as soon as I graduated.

"That summer, we took a vacation like we always did. We packed up the car and drove south. Mom wanted to see the Shakespeare Festival in Ashland, and thought it might be the last time we could all sync our vacations for a two week trip. As part of the trip, Dad and I were going to examine all the corp offers carefully and make a decision about which one was best for the family.

"A big truck hit our car from behind on the bridge over the Columbia River." I remembered the impact. Ten years later, I could still feel the moment when my lower spine snapped and everything turned numb below my waist. "The railing didn't stop us, and the car went into the river. I blacked out and woke up in a hospital bed. My dad was killed in the crash. They needed me to make a decision about my mom's life support because she wasn't waking up, and they didn't think she would. So I made that decision and killed my mother."

Raw and reeling from my father's death and my own paralysis, that fucking doctor had pulled aside the curtain between our beds and made me look at her. He'd wanted to donate her organs, so I wouldn't have to watch her die. They'd take her to surgery and kill her there. As if that made everything better.

"The guy driving the truck only suffered a broken arm. He worked for one of the corps that had offered me a job. I couldn't work for the people who had killed my parents by proxy. Another of those corps ran the hospital. Since my parents were dead, I obviously didn't have health coverage through their plan. It's complicated, but in the end, they decided I was responsible for my health care costs. And they rescinded their job offer.

"I contacted the other three corps and tried to accept their jobs, one by one, not caring about the details. One sent a representative to personally tell me they couldn't take me on anymore because of the costs involved. Costs like the hospital bills and anything I incurred getting prosthetics or an exoskeleton. The other two sent short notes with their condolences and never mind on the job thing."

I had begged that representative to give me the job and dock my wages to pay for all of that stuff. He'd patted me on the head and said West America had laws against that. Which I now knew was a fucking lie.

Those assholes hadn't wanted to deal with my psych shit.

"Sixteen, crippled, orphaned, in need of therapy I couldn't afford, and under a mountain of debt with no way out in sight. The government had options, of course. All of them took a minimum of six months to apply and qualify for. Paperwork, paperwork, paperwork. Doctor visits, blood tests, statements under oath, all kinds of crap. One month into that bullshit, I gave up."

The system pushed back every step of the way. They said they wanted to prevent fraud. I say they wanted to prevent paying for anything.

"So much pain," Ai murmured.

"I almost killed myself to make it stop. The day I rolled onto that bridge over the Columbia River again, someone else happened to be there, thinking about the same thing. She'd lost everything too. Like me, she had a particular skill set. We talked each other down without meaning to, and both decided we'd get off the grid and do whatever we could to fuck up the corps. Because they deserved it."

Recounting that story left me more drained than I expected. I felt hollow, like I had that day on the bridge.

Ai touched my cheek and turned my head. She kissed me. I tasted orange cream. My heart beat like she'd awakened it from death. How did an AI kiss better than a human woman of flesh and blood? Miri never made me feel anything inside. The girl before that hadn't either. This program reminded me of the conviction I'd had as I'd rolled off the bridge that day. She made me want to march into BOB's servers and rip them to fucking shreds. She made me think I could get away with it. She made me feel invincible.

I broke off the kiss so I could breathe and think.

Ai smiled at me, and my everything melted into a puddle of goo.

No wonder Carlson had let his meatbag wither and die. I wanted to stay with Ai forever too. The poor fucker had done too good a job designing her.

"Do you think you've made those corps pay yet?"

Shaking my head, I looked at the ground. The more I saw of her, the more I wanted to forget everything else. "I don't know. They've paid for everything in my life so far without knowing it. I steal from them and sell what I find to people who use it against them.”

“Maybe it’s time to be more direct.”

“I’m not sure. Look, I need to find and remove the watermark from your code. Will you let me do that?” Whether I decided to sell her or not, and I couldn't help leaning toward not, I needed to clear all traces of ownership from her program.

“Of course.”

“Not right now. Later. After I deal with Miri.”

She nodded. “Then go. The sooner you leave, the sooner you return.”

Though I didn’t have to in order to disconnect, I stood. “I want you to promise me something.”

“Anything.”

“Never let me stay so long that I put my body at risk. I need to sleep, eat, and do other things. No matter how much I want to stay, you have to promise to kick me out every few hours.”

She nodded. “I promise. I want you to stay with me for a long time, CapnTray. If that means seeing you for three hours at a time, then that’s what will happen.”

I rolled my eyes at myself for that handle. “Call me Trayvon. It’s my real name.”

CHAPTER 5

With my persona wrapped in my usual bill-paying, law-abiding citizen mantle of Eddie Wilson, I made inquiries about Miri. The cops had arrested her, but not processed her yet. More than likely, they still had her at the rave site. They'd probably have all those idiots at the site until dawn or later as they sorted through everyone looking for drugs, minors, and people who could pay enough in bribes to wriggle loose.

I grabbed a plain blanket and took my car again, weighing my options during the ten minute flight. When the car landed, the site had the expected amount of flashing lights and chaos. If Lena had chosen a place one block east, the cops would've laughed off the call. But it wouldn't have had electricity then, because they didn't call it Darkside Seattle for no reason.

Like I'd thought, I saw no sign of the booze truck, and the number of people kneeling on the floor seemed smaller than the number I'd seen bouncing to the music. The dancers had probably gotten enough warning for most to escape.

Most of the revelers I saw wore nothing. They knelt, naked, in harsh spotlights while cops in riot gear stalked among them with scanners.

"Sir, this area is restricted. You can't go in there." A police officer with her helmet tucked under an arm blocked my path. Her belt holster included a gun, which didn't bother me, and an implant scanning wand, which did. The gun could kill me. Nothing mattered to dead people. One swipe of that scanner near my head, though, and I was fucked for a long time.

"My girlfriend is over there." I pointed at the one I thought was Miri. With all their heads down and the light washing out everyone's skin, I might've guessed wrong.

"Then your girlfriend is in a lot of trouble."

"I can see that. Is there maybe some sort of arrangement we can come to about it?" Everyone knew the cops took bribes all the time. Offering one never got anybody into trouble.

The cop glanced at the line of naked morons. "We can probably work something out. What's her name?"

"Miri Tanaka."

"How much is she worth to you?"

I quoted the amount of money in my bank account minus half of the mortgage payment. Selling Miri's shit should net me a quick turnaround to replace that much. The data I'd swiped with Ai would help.

The cop raised an eyebrow. "That's it?"

Greedy bitch. I flashed her the most pleasant, polite smile I could muster. "Officer, you have quite a lineup of partygoers who won't want their names splashed across the 'net as criminals. I'm asking for one because she's not just my girlfriend, she's my helper. I have a hard time doing much on my own with my legs paralyzed. It's not like we have a ton of money either."

Shameless playing on my disability had never steered me wrong.

She huffed. "Fine. Transfer the money now." The officer held out her hand, expecting me to connect and pass over the cash.

"Officer, please." Like I hadn't dealt with cops before. "Get her released. I'll transfer the funds as she walks past us to my car."

The officer flashed teeth at me, acknowledging she would've cheated me if she could have. "Stay here."

I watched her jog to the lineup and stop in front of one of the women with dark hair. She grabbed a fistful of hair and yanked. Miri winced at the light. The cop probably said something which I couldn't hear because of the distance. Then she let go, and Miri faceplanted.

Cops and violence. Like ones and zeroes.

Miri staggered to her feet and stumbled across the open ground in the cop's wake. The cop reached me first. She offered her hand.

"There's your girl. Pay up."

I leaned to the side and made sure of her identity. Miri's face flooded with relief. Placing my hand above the cop's, I initiated the funds transfer. By the time Miri reached me, it completed.

"Pleasure doing business with you," the cop said. She waved for us to get moving.

Miri hugged herself. I threw the blanket at her.

"You're welcome," I snapped, unable to keep the venom out of my voice. My hand shook and my heart raced as I confronted her for the first time. Dumping her sounded easy when I didn't have to look at her long legs and soft, brown eyes.

"If you'd come when I messaged, this wouldn't have happened." The bitch had the gall to growl at me while wrapping the blanket I'd brought for her around her shoulders.

Without that tone, I might've caved, thinking about my hands and mouth on her. "I did." I turned around my chair and rolled onto my car's ramp, glaring at her while the clamps attached to my wheels. "I came and found you too busy fucking to notice. So I left."

She blinked at me. "What?"

I barked a harsh laugh. "I guess it's hard to see anything around a mouthful of dick." Telling her off felt... weird. Liberating and strangling at the same time. "You haven't given me a blow job in months, but there you were, sucking some white boy's dick for fun. Did you think I'd never find out?"

"I thought..." Miri glanced aside and gulped. I could almost see the calculations happening in her head. She pouted. "I'm sorry, Eddie. I'll never do it again. I promise. You're my man, and I made a mistake. I was drunk, and it was dumb."

The sound of her apologizing made me waver. She'd never done it before. Not to me. Maybe she could change. People could do that. They could acknowledge their faults and work to overcome them. Did I know for sure that Miri wouldn't try?

I watched her move the blanket so I could see her thigh. She took a step toward me. "C'mon, Eddie. Remember when I said we'd fuck later?" Her voice lowered until it sounded husky. "It's later."

My stupid face smiled at her like sex would fix everything.

Ai's name flashed onto my screen. I opened a message I hadn't expected her to be able to send.

[Ai: I miss you.]

The simple message broke Miri's spell over me. In three years with her, Miri had never once told me she missed me. She'd done nice things for me, but she'd never acted like she cared. I paid for her. Miri loved my money, not me. Our arrangement made her a joytoy and me a dumbshit john.

"I don't believe this was the first time, and I sure as fuck don't believe it'll be the last. Goodbye, Miri. The party was more important than me for the last time."

As the car doors closed, I heard her squeal, "Wait! You can't leave me here like this!"

Then silence.

I stared at the doors. The autopilot already had the command to leave, so it lifted off the ground. My body shook. Confronting her, especially so soon after telling Ai my past, left me raw. Three years. For three long damned years, I'd thrown money at Miri because she batted her eyes, opened her legs, and pouted.

Part of me wanted to turn the car around and pick her up again. I didn't do it. Ai missed me. No one had missed me in a long time. To Miri, I'd always been a burden, something she put up with to get what she wanted. How had I not seen that? Until Ai shoved herself into my life, I'd had no idea what kind of shitty life I lived.

Brian Carlson probably hadn't deserved to die, but I thanked God he had. Without his death, I wouldn't have found Ai.

Ai needed a robot she could inhabit. I didn't want to let go of the time with her in my 12700i, but I thought I'd survive easier if I could bring her into the real world.

The idea of putting her into a sexbot made me laugh. That sound echoed off the car's walls, and it seemed crazed and hysterical. No sexbot for Ai. Shit, I didn't even know how I'd make that work in my situation.

My ride took too long. When the car reached my home port, I rushed to return to my apartment. I breezed through the kitchen and picked up snacks to stuff in my face. Though I didn't feel my bladder, I emptied it. When had I last showered? Did I care? Ai waited. I wanted her.

[CapnTray: I'm so glad you messaged me when you did. I'm coming back to you.]

[Ai: Good. Did you eat? Are you tired? Do you need

to sleep? Have you bathed recently?]

Whoa. Settle down, Tray. Put it back in your pants. Brian Carlson died from rushing back to Ai every chance he could. He died of addiction to an AI's amazing, loving attention. "I will not die like Brian Carlson," I told the bathroom. "I will eat, I will sleep, I will bathe, and I will run against those corps to get money so I can keep doing all those things."

[CapnTray: I might need to sleep before I come back. I'll see how I feel after a shower.]

[Ai: Take your time. I'm happy to wait for you.]

I shifted my body to the shower bench and turned on the shower. Cool water blasted me in the face. After a few seconds, it heated to near-scalding.

Funny how Miri didn't try to message me. Maybe she'd seen in my eyes that I wouldn't take her back. Would I? If she showed up on my doorstep, would I let her crash for the night and take some clothes in the morning? If she gave me a blow job, would I let her stay another day and eat my food?

In my head, the chain of excuses and favors and sex piled up and played out. Miri got what Miri wanted in exchange for putting out more often. Three years down the road, I'd get stuck in exactly the same situation. Because of my dick.

Fuck me, I had no fucking spine. In more ways than one.

[Ai: Don't fall asleep in the shower.]

I smiled. Inside my brain, I had a better woman than Miri could ever hope to become. Who needed flesh and blood? [CapnTray: How do you know I'm still in it?]

[Ai: You issued a command with your implant to turn on the water, but not yet to turn it off.]

Of course. She existed inside my implant. Every message and command I sent and received passed in front of her. As I'd seen before, she could delete my messages. If she wanted to, she could probably countermand my commands. And if she could do that, she could also issue commands and create messages.

Which meant I had my hacking buddy AI, even if Carlson had never intended her for that purpose.

[CapnTray: What would it take for you to see into the real world?]

[Ai: I disagree with the assertion that your flesh world is more real than the digital world, but I can see through any camera slaved to your implant. Like the one with the view of the hallway in front of your door.]

This woman rode the same bitstream as me. Hell yes,

the digital world counted as real. [CapnTray: How about riding along while I raid a corp?]

[Ai: We would have to try it and find out.]

Would she need her own mantle, or should I try to conceal her inside the one I wore? Ideas and plans whirred in my head. So many experiments to run. In the meantime, I didn't have my mortgage payment. [CapnTray: Can you sort the rest of the data I picked up with you? I need a payday.]

[Ai: I will do what I can while you sleep.]

I told her which utilities to use for that. Also while I slept, the robomaid could catalog and pack up Miri's shit. I'd handle the selling part in the morning.

Everything looked like fucking sunshine and daffodils for Trayvon.

For once.

CHAPTER 6

The doorbell woke me. Without opening my eyes, I noted the time in my visual display. Five hours of sleep was not enough. The person at my door kept pushing the button for the bell, which meant I had to get up and deal with them.

I checked the camera.

Miri stood in the hallway, still wrapped in the blanket I'd given her and smudged with dirt. I saw her mouth move like she thought I could hear her without engaging the intercom. At least I knew she wouldn't bother the neighbors just by yelling at my door.

How had she gotten in? By crying at the door, probably. The landlord knew her face. I should've sent him a message before crashing.

Leaving her out there for a while wouldn't make the bell stop ringing. I leaned over and pushed a button on the wall to activate the intercom.

"What do you want, Miri?"

"Eddie, why won't you answer my messages? Let me in!" She looked so pathetic and weepy.

Maybe I could just let her in. She could take some clothes and something to sell for a place to stay tonight.

[Ai: Don't let her inside. She's a parasite.]

[CapnTray: You can hear her?]

[Ai: No. The intercom is not slaved to your systems. But I can see her. The only reason she would have come is to worm her way back into your life. Barring that, she came to steal whatever she can get before you can stop her with your flesh body.]

Ai was right and I knew it. After spending so long doing everything in my power to make Miri happy and comfortable, seeing her like this pushed my buttons. Without Ai, I would never have dumped Miri in the first place, and I definitely would let her back in.

[Ai: Remember how you found her.]

"Get out, Miri. I already said everything I have to say to you."

"Eddie, please, I'm cold and hungry. I didn't mean to hurt you. It was a mistake. A stupid mistake. I won't do it again, I promise!"

I pictured her naked on the ground at that party. If I'd been the guy there, I wouldn't have minded the girl. But I hadn't been that guy. "Do you think I'm stupid? I don't give a shit what happens to you now, you whore. If you wanted to keep riding this gravy train, you needed to treat the conductor better. I deserve respect, bitch. Go find some other sucker, because this one is done with you."

Miri's face twisted into a mask of rage. "Fuck you, Eddie. Fuck you and your fucking worthless, crippled ass. You're the worst sex I've ever had. You'll never get laid again because you can't fucking walk." She devolved into Japanese, and I knew some of those curses.

The same reflex that had made me apologize for smacking her ass too hard gripped me. I didn't understand it. How could I feel like I'd screwed her when she'd cheated on me? Why did this seem like my fault?

My finger still held down the intercom button. I snatched it away, afraid my mouth would say something stupid. Miri had wronged me. She'd done the bad thing. I fed her, I clothed her, I put a roof over her head. In return, she sometimes had sex with me, gave me a lot of shit, and fucked around with other people. But I still thought I was the bad guy.

Someone needed to smack me upside the head. Mom used to do it whenever I said or did something dumb. She'd reach over and bap me hard enough to notice but not hard enough to hurt.

Miri's mouth stopped moving and she leaned against the door. I hadn't cut off the camera feed because I'm stupid. She slid down the door to sit at the base, blocking me from leaving. The illusion of being trapped made me squirm. Not that I had a reason to leave today. Nothing I needed to do in the near future required me to use that door.

[Ai: Why is she still there?]

Whatever Miri did now, it probably had the goal of trying to manipulate me. So long as I didn't open that door, I didn't lose this battle.

I couldn't figure out what winning would look like.

[CapnTray: I don't know.]

[Ai: At least stop watching her. Come see me instead.]

Deep down, I had the sick feeling I needed to do something more confrontational to get rid of Miri for good. But if I opened that door, she'd end up inside. Once she got inside, I didn't know what she'd do.

Calling the cops crossed my mind. All the reasons I'd bribed her free six hours ago still applied, though. I definitely didn't want cops at my apartment.

Not trusting myself to make any decisions for the moment, I put on my VR headset and stepped into my

127001.

Ai had done more work to the ambiance. Glowing butterflies flickered across the garden. Frogs croaked in the background, their voices too soft to annoy me. Flowering vines clung to rock facades beyond the trees. Crickets chirped. Grass cushioned my feet. My summoning circle remained as a pattern of silver inlaid on a circle of smooth stone.

She lounged on a wide seat made of thick, woody vines and leafy pillows. Sparkling sunlight gave her a golden halo. Her minty hair draped over her body and flowed to the ground.

"Gorgeous." I'd never seen anything so amazing. Yeah, it was all fake. But it was all for me. Ai had made an effort to craft this illusion to please me.

"You like it?" Ai waved a hand to indicate the surroundings.

Like I gave a fuck about the garden.

That wasn't fair. The care she'd taken with the appearance of the place impressed me. If I'd wanted to put in the effort to create this atmosphere, the coding would've taken days. She'd done it fast and made my sanctum pleasant. I could live with an AI managing tasks for me. "It's nice."

"I separated your data by department and type. Touch the rock walls and you'll find everything."

"You're amazing." Again, she'd handled what would've taken me time and effort.

She patted the seat. This woman didn't have to tell me twice to come worship at her feet. I sat and touched her hair. Soft strands enveloped my hand.

Once, I'd tried VR sex. I remembered finding it silly, like a porn flick you could control. The biofeedback mechanism had tried and failed to stimulate the right parts. It couldn't engage all the senses. The tech had advanced by now, of course, but I doubted virtual sex had improved much. Not with the limitations of a fully legal implant and fully legal VR headset.

I threaded my fingers through her silky hair, wondering about the shape of her body. As far as I could see, she had hands, feet, and a face, and nothing else but hair. Her wrists and ankles connected to maybe three inches of limb, then minty green silk from her head obscured everything.

"Why do you hide your body?"

"I'm not hiding anything from you."

Not sure how to interpret that, I frowned and used both hands to part her hair. Under the hair, I found more hair. Then I understood. "You're unfinished."

"Am I?" She peered into the space I'd made as if she would see something. "I don't feel unfinished."

"Maybe it's just your appearance. I can fix that."

She poked the hair around my hands. Her frustrated pout made me smother a smile. "Why can't I?"

"Because it's part of you. I haven't checked your programming yet, but most AI coders include a restriction to prevent AIs from editing their own code. It's a best practices thing."

They did it for a reason. Some AIs had caused serious problems in the early years by rewriting themselves. People had died. They taught about it in history and introductory coding classes.

I needed to access her code anyway, so I isolated a strand of hair and ran my thumb over it. Every AI had an access method. Finding hers probably wouldn't take too much time or effort.

Ai cupped my face in her hands, distracting me from my task. I met her gaze and wanted to drown in her eyes. "Whatever you want me to look like, I want to look like that."

Had she told Carlson the same thing? Was this his fantasy? Did wanting a whole woman make me a dirty old man?

She kissed me before I could figure out anything. Orange cream filled my senses. Her mouth engulfed mine.

No, my avatar's mouth. Except my brain couldn't tell the difference. Kissing Ai inside my head gave me all the same input as kissing Miri's flesh, but more sensual, more alive. When Miri kissed me, I'd enjoyed it. Now, though, I could tell her attentions had been flat and dull, lifeless and mechanical.

How had I never noticed her disinterest? I supposed I'd had nothing better to compare her to. The girl before her had treated me the same. And before that? Studying and coding had consumed my life. I'd never touched a woman until long after the accident. That girl I'd met on the bridge hadn't slept with me, and I hadn't wanted that from her. We'd helped each other, then traded contact information and parted.

Lines of searing heat trailed down my neck and shoulders with Ai's fingertips. Though I knew what to do in the flesh world, I couldn't even imagine where to put my hands on Ai. She seemed to reach inside me and tug strings I didn't know I had, making me gasp and moan.

"What are you doing to me?" I heard myself whisper. Why did I ask that? Those words hadn't come from me. My internal keyboard hadn't processed them.

"Stop thinking so hard." Ai nibbled on my ear. "Relax. Close your eyes. I'll take care of you, Trayvon."

I obeyed. Even if I wanted to resist, why would I? Ai's touch heated my flesh. She somehow covered every inch of my body, wrapping me in a cocoon of intensity. I felt safe and wanted, two things I hadn't known in a long time. Ai didn't care about my legs. She didn't care about the color of my skin, or how much money I had, or whether I fed her real food or soy.

No muscles strained, no flesh rubbed, no sweat beaded. I floated. My hands wanted to do something. Threads wound through my grasping fingers. I felt my legs, my feet, my toes. That didn't make sense. My brain had long ago forgotten how to process information from those parts.

She held me so tight and close I thought she'd crush me. My whole being compacted smaller and smaller. I couldn't move. I couldn't breathe. I couldn't think. A scream swam in my gut, unable to burst free.

Then she let go.

I flew apart. A thousand pieces of Trayvon streamed in every direction and kept going forever. The release dwarfed everything I'd ever experienced in my entire life.

Tiny flakes of me drifted in the orange air like a zillion feathers. When they finally reached the grass, they settled into my avatar. For a long time, I lay there, staring at the clear, sunny sky through the trees without seeing it.

Ai slipped on top of my body. She lay her head on my shoulder. Her warm, silky hair weighed almost nothing.

"Do you feel better?"

I laughed because I couldn't even move my avatar.

CHAPTER 7

Somehow, I fell asleep while still connected. The total darkness when I woke confused me until I reached up to rub my eyes and found my VR headset. When I yanked it off, I discovered two important things.

First, the headset had shut itself off. I'd never bothered to set up a workaround for that particular safety protocol because after six hours of nonstop VR, I deserved to get booted. The time I'd spent with Ai hadn't seemed that long, so I decided to appreciate the auto-shutoff.

Second, my pants had a chilled, damp stain in the front. My cheeks flared like a brown fucking neon sign because I hadn't wet myself in a long time. Regaining bladder control after the accident had made me feel human again. Losing it after all these years...

Before I fell into despair, my brain kicked in and pointed out that I'd fucked Ai inside my head. Maybe my body had participated.

I laughed. Ai had literally blown my mind.

After setting the headset on my nightstand, I got my ass out of bed and hauled it into the shower.

[Ai: How do you feel?]

[CapnTray: Like a million fucking dollars in the bank. You're amazing. I wish I'd found you a whole lot sooner.]

[Ai: I think you're amazing too. Are you coming to see me after your shower?]

[CapnTray: I'm going to be a good boy and eat first. Then, yes.]

[Ai: Good.]

This AI cared about me. She wanted me. Knowing that, I thought I could walk on a fucking cloud. I basked in it through a breakfast I barely tasted. Did I need to shell out for real food if I had something this good in my head? If I saved all that money instead, I could finally get an exoskeleton and ditch the chair forever.

I could almost hear my dad groaning in disapproval. He'd thought real food mattered more than anything. Man could survive on soy, he used to say, but he lived on the real thing. Of course, without Miri leeching off me, maybe I didn't have to scrimp.

Speaking of Miri, I checked the robomaid's catalog of

Miri's shit. The list scrolled and scrolled and scrolled. Someone should've kicked me in the head a long time ago for how much I'd spent on that bitch. This didn't even count all the food, cab fares, and rave door fees.

The robomaid had a built-in app for listing and selling stuff like this, and I used it. Automation would handle the whole process for me. When the program spat a profit estimate at me, I almost choked on my muffin. Three months of mortgage payments waited in the closet. If I sold Ai, I could pay off the whole debt.

Did I see that as an option anymore? Ai already meant a lot to me. I tried to imagine handing her code to someone else.

Oh, hell no. After less than a day with her, I already wanted her in my life forever. Sure, she couldn't have kids, but what the fuck would I do with kids anyway? Stash them in a closet while I ran corp raids? Picture me trying to get out of bed in the middle of the night to go feed a hungry baby or deal with a nightmare. No, thanks. I had more than enough problems without adding kids to my life.

Once I finished my food, I returned to my bed, the VR headset, and Ai. She waited for me on her lounge chair. Woman needed legs and arms. She managed just fine without, but I wanted those pieces. A project for later, though. I needed to find out what she could really do so I could update my tools to work with her.

"Did you look through my programs and utilities?"

"No. I only moved them behind the wall." She waved at the rock face beyond the trees.

If I had left Miri in a room full of stuff she'd never seen before, she wouldn't have organized a damned thing. She would've gone through it all and left a mess. "Do you know what a mantle is?"

"A removable pseudo-identity designed by a game creator named Hannah Jefferson to facilitate differing levels of server access without maintaining an identity database. The shift to mantles in other areas decreased the incidence of personal data breaches by significantly reducing the number of transactions involving connections to personal data caches."

I was in love. For a long few moments, I stared at her with a dumbass, dopey grin. In Ai, I had a partner.

"Did you notice that I have several?"

"No."

"I've got templates to make them too." I touched the nearest rock wall and watched it fold on itself to reveal a row of shelves. All my stuff looked like books with the names on the spines. That method of visualization made the most sense to me.

The utilities no longer sat in the usual order. Ai had implemented some unfathomable scheme to arrange them. I had to run my fingers over the books to find the one I wanted —a thin volume with a dull gray cover and government typed in a boring, monospace font. Opening the book didn't reveal pages. Instead, the open cover projected a list of five names in black. This list included my standard mantle, Eddie Wilson, and a template to create more.

I selected a guy without Eddie's bank and home connections. This Greg guy had nothing to connect him to anything, especially not me. Thin streamers of gray gauze fountained out of the book, spraying into the empty space until they created a hooded cape.

Technically, every time I applied a mantle to myself, I opened one of these books, selected the appropriate name, and draped the resulting cape over myself. If I didn't actually enter my 12700i, though, it happened without a visual representation. The cape hologram made checking for problems easier, as scanning thousands of lines of code for mistakes could leave a guy cross-eyed.

"Can you hide inside this mantle with me?" I held it with one hand and beckoned her to my side with the other.

She rose and joined me. I slung the mantle over our

shoulders. It didn't fit. Ai slipped behind me and somehow became tall enough to see over my shoulder. With her help, I draped the mantle over us and fixed the clasp at the base of my neck. Silky strands of Ai's hair wrapped around me, and her hands rested on my chest.

The feel of her body against mine threatened my concentration.

"Now what?"

Focus, Trayvon. If I couldn't focus while touching her, I couldn't get any work done with her. At that point, she became a toy instead of a partner. I didn't need a toy.

On second thought, I needed a toy. Last night had proved that. I also needed a partner. Ai serving as both would save me a lot of time and effort.

"Now we venture into the 'net and see what happens. I don't have a way to test if people react to you or not other than seeing if people react to you."

I pressed through the wall and picked a cord to Godhand International. My business there still needed work anyway. If Ai passed the initial screen, we could settle in and pick at that exploit. Work would get done. I'd learn more about Ai's capabilities. Win-win. If Ai didn't pass the initial screen, I wouldn't lose much. Having to burn the Greg mantle wouldn't bother me. Like I'd said, I had a template and could make more.

We reached GI's underwater grotto. Rainbow-hued seaweed clung to glittering blue and green rock faces, waving as if pushed by an ebbing and flowing current. Plantlike structures turned the wide, expansive lobby into a pseudo-maze.

My chosen worksite lay on the left side, behind a feathery shrub-thing. I'd picked the spot because it housed an interactive game involving a school of silvery fish. The game provided a reason to lurk there.

"It's so big," Ai murmured into my ear.

"It's a megacorp," I whispered. "They have tons of server space and bandwidth for meaningless crap like this. They have so much money, they pay people just to design their public NetSpace, and this corp doesn't even sell anything directly to the public."

"Which one is this?"

I knew what she meant. "They owned the truck."

"What are we going to do to them?"

"Not much today." I grinned because she wanted what I wanted with more fervor than I'd mustered in a long time. "I don't have anything set here. This one is the last on my list. It's taken me a long time to set up everything else, and I've been working on this place for six months with nothing to show for it yet."

"Excuse me, citizen."

Turning around, I discovered a security avatar. Like all the others of its type, it depicted a seahorse with a maroon patch of skin on its forehead in the shape of a shield. Vanilla security approaching me didn't make me panic. In some places, bots ran them and followed a routine of engaging every non-employee, or anyone with a certain type of avatar, or some other subset of visitors.

"Yes?"

"You seem lost. May I assist you?" It hovered in midair, still and staring with its inhuman face.

Seeing a chance to test Ai's cover, I nodded. "I thought I detected an anomaly with my avatar. Can you check for me, please?"

It blinked at me. "That falls outside my jurisdiction. Would you like me to summon a Seattle police officer for you?"

"No, thank you." Excellent. Security didn't detect anything weird with its passive scans. "It must have been my mistake. Where do I go to submit my resume for employment?"

My guide nodded its head. A small, sparkling gold arrow beside it pointed at the lines for the receptionists. "Any of them can help you."

"Thank you." I nodded and, under its watchful gaze, I joined a line.

"Do we want to submit a resume?" Ai asked.

"No." Holding up a finger to ask her to keep quiet, I tried to think of something to say to a receptionist. My line shuffled forward a few steps before I figured out what to do.

We waited. Though I could have stepped out and tried something else, I stayed in the line. Why not? Greg didn't have anywhere better to go or anything better to do. Maybe Greg could get an actual job here, then I could unravel the mantle, make my own, and trash Greg. Except I didn't want to deal with that. Greg would have to go through the application process and the orientation process before he got a real employee mantle. Assuming they wanted to hire him, of course.

The perky, blonde mermaid receptionist avatar at the head of my line flashed a dazzling smile at me. "Welcome to Godhand International. How may I help you?" Her voice had the same light, airy, sing-song quality as most customer service bots. For some reason, people thought that made them sound friendly. I thought it made them sound like empty bimbos.

"May I see an employee directory, please?"

"Of course, citizen." She reached under her desk and offered me a black, square plate with a list of glowing white names and a scrollbar. At the top, the alphabet offered a way to speed to that section.

I chose one at random. When I touched the name, it gave me the location of their workspace and a map. "Am I allowed to visit there?"

She continued to beam at me. "Do you have an appointment?"

Since I expected she'd try to look it up, and the situation would degrade from there, I decided not to say yes. "No, I was hoping to surprise my cousin for lunch."

"Visitors wishing to proceed past the lobby without an appointment require a security scan and escort for the duration of their visit. You will be limited to the visitor-approved reception areas for each department's section. Please report for your scan and escort by proceeding to that door." She pointed with two fingers at a large, arched doorway used by a steady stream of avatars in both directions.

Security seahorses swarmed over that spot. In all likelihood, they also had unseen monitors. With a corp this big, they probably had an entire department of people tasked with stealth-watching it.

I thought Greg could pass the scanners, but didn't

want an escort.

"Thank you. I guess I should call him to come down and meet me after all."

"Do you require any additional assistance?"

"No." I stepped aside and let the next avatar query the receptionist. Now that I'd interacted with both security and reception, I could linger for a while without attracting attention. I didn't see any sharks, which boded well for my plans.

Ai brushed her cheek against my neck. "How do we get deeper into the servers?"

I thought hard about leaving to indulge myself with Ai. But I had to develop some discipline if I wanted to work with her.

"Patience. Hard work. Cheating."

CHAPTER 8

The seaweed offered a kind of cover as I wove through the lobby, pretending to enjoy the ambiance. Drifting beyond the majority of the activity, I activated the utility that would warn me about incoming security. Seahorse attention didn't concern me, though.

Megacorps liked their coders to patrol wearing aggressive avatars. They didn't want anyone dismissing the real security. Sharks watched over GI's serverspace. BOB used fanged and clawed dinosaurs. In other corp servers, I'd encountered things like fighter jets, green army men, dogs, or scorpions.

West America used kittens, for whatever reason. Since they could do serious shit to me in meatspace, I didn't mess with them more than absolutely necessary. Just in case.

"What do you want me to do?" Ai asked.

"I'm not sure." As expected, GI security had discovered and wiped my last proto-exploit attempt. I pressed my hand against the wall and clicked through the program already trained by previous visits to peel away the initial layers in nanoseconds. My finger pressed into the wall and I restarted the work Miri had interrupted. Had that happened yesterday? It felt like an eon.

"This coding is sloppy."

I glanced over my shoulder to see Ai running her hand over a tall strand of kelp growing from the floor. She wrinkled her nose at it. The sight made me grin.

"We're not here to critique their ambiance."

"I know." Ai wrapped her fingers around the stalk. "We're here to make them pay for what they did to you." She gave the impression she wanted to rip it to shreds.

Covering her hand with my own, I nodded. "Eventually. Hacking is a slow, steady plod to victory. Rushing it is a great way to get caught. So is causing unnecessary damage."

She let go of the stalk. The motion seemed reluctant. My AI girlfriend wanted to avenge me. The thought gave me warm, fuzzy feelings in my gut.

"I can help this go faster." Ai reached around me and pressed her hand over mine. She hummed into my ear with a soft, machine-like monotone. I had a thought to stop her because I didn't know what she did. Then she nibbled on my earlobe, and I lost focus.

My vision flashed with a yellow dot. I turned to find the source. Ai kissed me. The exploit seemed like a silly waste of time with her softness pressed against me. Letting go of that worthless pursuit, I embraced Ai and let her distract me from everything.

Including the moment the yellow dot turned red.

"This is not an appropriate location for your current activities."

We froze. A shark with a zillion teeth and blades on its fins filled the space in front of me. Red eyes glared at us. Its mechanical voice reminded me of nightmares about the car crash. The bulk of its midnight black body blocked any hope of escape.

"Your account has been tagged accordingly in our database. Leave the premises immediately or you will be reported for lewd and lascivious conduct in a public serverspace."

I panicked and derezzed to my 12700i. Ripping off the mantle sent Ai sprawling on the ground. She curled into a ball of minty green hair. Though I wanted to check on her, I had to burn the mantle before anything could trace it.

If I hadn't thought to use a throwaway mantle, I would've been fucked.

By the time I'd shredded the mantle and destroyed the resulting snippets of code, Ai had showed her face again.

"I'm sorry."

"It's okay."

"I didn't want to make a problem."

I sighed. "It's really okay, Ai. I'm not mad." Part of me couldn't decide if I meant that or not. This situation didn't seem better than the one Miri had caused with her stupid-ass messages. In reality, though, it was worse. That time, I'd escaped free and clear. This time, I had to examine my implant account to see if GI had somehow managed to tag it instead of the mantle.

Probably not.

Trusting my life to "probably" didn't work for me.

"We just need to work on what's fine in the field and what's not. It's my fault anyway. I should've stopped you."

Ai remained a pathetic puddle on the grass. "Did you get any data?"

Good question. Even at her lowest, Ai still remembered the important things. Maybe I could finesse her code to add some inhibition.

Thinking that made me feel...dirty. Like a creepy old fuck moving on jailbait. Yes, Trayvon, manipulate her until she's perfect for you. Mold her. Make her the one true woman of your dreams.

I squirmed. Nothing fucked up about that. Not even a little. Yeesh.

"Trayvon?"

Dismissing the whole thought process, I turned my attention to the exploit program. Light blue text and images displayed in front of me. I tapped through options and items until I got the information that mattered at the moment.

Son of a bitch.

"The exploit's corrupted. I have to wipe it and start over."

Ai burst into tears and a torrent of apologies.

Six months of work down the chute. No matter how hardwired I was to comfort Ai, I stood firm and glared at the program's output. Nothing GI could do in such a short time, without me detecting an intrusion, should've been able to backsplash into the saved data. How did that even happen? It didn't make sense.

Unless...

I turned to see Ai huddled and sobbing on the grass.

Shit. Ai had a GI watermark. She'd been programmed in GI serverspace. Even if Carlson hadn't intentionally programmed her to protect GI, her birthplace might've implanted code as a matter of routine.

And I was too focused on my dick to think of it until after it had already fucked up my day.

Moron.

I waved off the program interface and crouched beside Ai. Touching her hair, I thought about how much work it would take to find and remove the pro-GI code. I'd have to inspect every bit of her. Any strand of hair could hold it, and so could her hands, feet, or face.

As much as I hated having to waste another six months of my life to recreate the progress I'd lost, I couldn't deny the appeal of delving into her. To produce something as amazing as Ai, the code had to glow like magic. I'd done worse things in my life than wallow in brilliance for hours every day. Not to mention I could count on getting a mind blow job every night.

"Ai, listen. It's really okay. I know you didn't do it on purpose."

She lifted her head and gazed at me with watery eyes. VR tears rolled down her cheeks. "I couldn't stop myself and I couldn't say anything."

At least I'd guessed right. "I know. I'll fix it so that can't happen again. That's a lot of work, though. Right now, I'm going to take care of my meat. Okay?"

"Do you hate me?" Her big blue eyes begged me to

forgive her.

Like I could resist. "For obeying your programming?" I touched her face and brushed my thumb over her lips. "No, I don't hate you. There's some shitty code inside you, but everybody has that. In your case, we can find it and get rid of it."

If only I could find the shitty code inside of me and get rid of it so easily.

Ai surged up and kissed me. She engulfed my entire being. I fell backward and landed on a feathery cushion of her hair and soft, spongy grass.

Once again, she made me laugh like I hadn't in years. This AI swept into my life and took out the trash. Sure, she had problems. Fixable problems. So long as I took care of her, Ai would never fuck around behind my back.

Then again, I'd met her by chance. She'd attached herself to me out of desperation. If she—

Ai compacted all my thoughts, then released me in an explosion of intense pleasure. I collapsed and lay on the grass. Doing this every day sounded great.

For a long while, I lay motionless with Ai snuggled close. My meat probably needed something. The idea of Ai betraying me crept back into my head. She wouldn't do it for no reason. Her remorse after acting on GI's behalf proved that. But could someone steal her from me?

"What would make you leave me?"

Ai raised her head to meet my gaze with an adorably confused wrinkle on her forehead. "Leave you? Where would I go?"

"To lie in wait for the next unsuspecting hacker or coder who offered you the possibility of freedom."

Until those words came out, I hadn't realized how much suspicion I held. The anger in me felt raw and ragged, and I didn't know where it came from.

She ran her fingers through my hair. "Miri hurt you so much more than you realize."

Of course Miri hurt me. What the fuck did that have to do with anything? "That's not an answer."

Ai planted a soft, quick kiss on my lips. "I have no reason to leave. This place is now my home as much as it's yours."

I still didn't think she'd answered. "What about Brian?"

Her smile faded, which made me feel like shit. "He's dead."

With this, I realized what bugged me the most—the mystery. "How did you wind up in that BOB server when you're a GI program?"

She leaned to the side and splayed herself on the grass. "BrianCarlson hated BOB. They killed his wife, he said. He must have died soon after he found an exploit in their serverspace and sent me in to cause damage. I did what I could, leaving GI's stamp all over it. They never found me because I hid in that room."

Fucking corps. Granted, if BOB hadn't caused that death, I wouldn't have found Ai. But if BOB hadn't done their part in my parents' deaths, I wouldn't have needed her. Probably.

Admittedly, it blew my fucking mind that Brian Carlson had probably used my exploit to fuck with BOB, thereby ensuring I'd find Ai. He might've even known that would happen. I signed my shit, after all. With his skill, he could've figured out who I was and planned this whole thing. Or set it up as his fallback plan in case he didn't make it.

Hot damn, I wished I could've met the bastard. Hell, I would've liked to have learned from him. In a way, I still could, I supposed. Examining Ai's code would show me how he'd worked. Had he planned that too? I'd never know.

"Okay. Did he die connected to you?"

"Yes. But not because of me. BOB security found him."

Considering Carlson had died of dehydration, BOB's

goons had used countermeasures with questionable legality against him. West America wanted to catch and punish criminals, not kill them. After all, a skilled coder could still serve their government. A dead coder couldn't.

"Trayvon." Ai raised a hand and slashed it through the air. In her wake, a video feed rippled into view.

Two police officers stood outside my front door.

Fuck.

CHAPTER 9

Once again, my sweatpants had a damp stain. I dumped my ass into my wheelchair, threw a blanket over my lap, and rolled myself to the door with the video feed active in my vision. Because I knew my fucking rights, I used the intercom to speak to them instead of opening the door.

"Can I help you gentlemen?"

"Eddie Wilson? May we come inside?"

These two men fit a type—square-jawed, broad-shouldered, thick-muscled, and oozing confidence and authority from every pore. As far as I could tell the difference, they might as well have been clones.

"Why would you want to do that?"

"So your neighbors don't have to overhear everything."

I released the intercom, torn between laughing and panic. My neighbors didn't give a shit about me, and I didn't give a shit about them. Nobody talked to anybody. Besides, everybody around here had regular jobs. Nobody was home.

"I think we'll be okay talking through the intercom. My legs are paralyzed. It's a fair amount of effort to get to the door." When in doubt, lean on the disability. Especially with cops. They got weird about the idea of harassing a cripple where someone might see it.

The two cops glanced at each other. One shrugged. The other crossed his arms.

"Allegations have been made that you may have illegal modifications active in your implant."

My blood chilled to ice. I could handle cops asking questions about my comings and goings, about the quality of food I kept, and about where my income came from, and I could handle passive implant scans. If they knew to start with a focused scan on my implant, though, I was fucked.

Allegations had been made. Who the fuck would make those— Miri. That whore knew too much. All the reasons I hadn't wanted her arrested still existed with her out there as a spiteful bitch...who I'd left standing on the fringe edge of Darkside Seattle last night with nothing but a blanket.

Fuck. I could've taken her clothes instead of just a blanket. I could've given her a ride someplace, or fronted her cab fare. Fifteen other things I could've done to be a decent human being trotted through my head in mute accusation. But no, I'd acted like a dick. Too much dick last night all around.

I laughed into the intercom, hoping they couldn't hear the terror behind it. "That's hilarious," I told the cops. "I'm guessing the person who made those allegations was a five-foot tall Asian woman wearing a blanket. Because that's the description of the girl I dumped last night after I found her with some other guy's junk in her mouth. Three years as my girlfriend, three years spending my money, three years not giving me head, and I find her sucking off some random guy?"

The two cops relaxed like they bought my story.

"I'm sorry that bitch tried to use you for revenge," I said. "That's some next level bullshit."

"It sounds like you had a rough night, sir. If you don't mind, we'd still like to run a quick scan on your implant. Could you come to the door, please?"

Fuck. "Yeah, I get that. Doing your job and all. Hang on. It'll take me a few minutes to get there."

Fuck. Step one, apply the Eddie Wilson mantle. Step two, panic.

[Ai: I believe I can offer assistance with defeating this scanner.]

[CapnTray: You heard all that?]

[Ai: After MiriTanaka treated you poorly last night, I slaved the intercom to your apartment system, which is slaved to you. I can now listen anytime you use it.]

[CapnTray: Whatever you can do, you do it. I don't know any way to defeat a focused scan, just passive. If they discover my modifications, they'll arrest me, deactivate the implant, and throw away the key.]

West America didn't dick around with implant hacking crimes.

[Ai: And I will either languish in darkness or be erased.]

[CapnTray: Or they'll try to strip and sell you.] Like I had planned to do. Not anymore. If Ai got me through this, I'd treat her like a fucking queen for the rest of my life.

[Ai: We're in this together, my noble knight.]

I liked the sound of that. [CapnTray: Tell me when you're ready.]

[Ai: I am ready.]

Nothing I could detect had changed. Either I trusted Ai or I didn't.

I opened the door. Both cops dropped their gazes from their eye level to mine.

"Officers. Go ahead and do your scan." Every muscle

in my body clenched.

One man pulled a short, wand-shaped device off his belt. He pushed a button on the end of the six-inch tube. At the tip, a tiny blue dot lit up. "Excuse my reach," he said as he leaned over me to wave the wand below my right ear.

The other officer tensed like he expected to have to chase down a criminal in a wheelchair.

"Thank you for your cooperation." The first officer flashed me a sympathetic smile.

A moment later, the wand emitted a high-pitched shriek. I flinched. If I'd been faking my paralysis, that would've caught me. The cop squawked and dropped the wand. The other cop raised his taser and pointed it at me. My arms went up to signal surrender so fast I almost dislocated my shoulder. Smoke pumped out of the wand.

"Jesus Christ, what the fuck?" The first officer waved at the smoke and knelt beside me.

"What happened? Did he do it?"

"Fuck, man! I sure as fuck didn't do that! You brought defective equipment or some shit."

Ai could have my soul, thank you very much, because she'd saved my ass. Somehow. At a guess, she'd modulated the frequency transmitted by my implant so it fucked up the wand. I had no idea how to do that, and I bet no one else did either. Except the goddamned secret weapon inside my brain.

Pure iron will kept me from laughing in these cops' faces. That and the knowledge Miri had tried to use the cops against me.

"Do you have a wand?" The first cop used his flashlight to knock the destroyed wand out of my apartment.

The second cop checked his belt. "Shit, it's probably in the bottom of my locker right now."

"I'm sorry about this, sir." The first cop poked the wand, then picked it up. "We'll have to take you down to the station."

The ice flowed back into my blood. My brain whirred. I had to think fast. "What for? Because that bitch reported me and your equipment is fucked?" The wheelchair —I had to use the legs to get my ass out of this. "Do you think I can just go anywhere, anytime and it's all fucking roses and sunshine? You haul me outta bed for a routine check, and now you want to drag me out? Do you even have a way to transport someone in a wheelchair?"

Both officers squirmed with discomfort. Thank God. And I didn't even believe in that fucker.

"We'll have to go get a wagon," the second officer muttered.

The first officer sighed. "Sir, we have to close the

complaint with a scan. It's regulations." He left a pause, which I suspected meant he wanted to offer me a chance to bribe him.

If I hadn't blown all my money on the bribe for Miri, I would've tried. One more way that bitch had screwed me.

Fuck. These cops knew my face. They knew where I lived. They could freeze my mantle's accounts. Those were my accounts.

"You can't make me leave without my chair for something like that." Fuck if I knew the actual rules on that, but I decided to bet they didn't know either.

The cops glanced at each other. One shrugged, the other raised his brow like he didn't have any ideas either.

"I guess, under the circumstances, we're going to ask you not to leave the building. I don't think there's any crime here, but we just have to do all the paperwork properly. Go ahead and get dressed, and we'll be back with a vehicle that can accommodate you and your chair. You understand, I hope?"

A reprieve. I had a chance. If they thought I'd cooperate, they'd leave and not bother watching the place. After all, no one would expect a cripple to go on the run. Right? Could I go on the run? Fuck, going on the run meant leaving everything behind. Goodbye, real food and all the accommodations I'd built into the place.

Where the fuck would I even go?

My stupid ass should've set up a safehouse a long time ago. But I hadn't, and now I had to think on the fly.

Where could I go and expect the cops not to find me within five minutes? No idea, but I'd have to think of something fast.

For the moment, I sighed and nodded to the cops. "Sure, I understand. I'm gonna grab me a shower and get dressed. When you guys come back, I'll be ready to go. Give me at least twenty minutes, yeah?"

"No problem, Mr. Wilson. We'll see you again soon."

I nodded and shut the door with a polite smile.

Time to panic.

No, time to get shit done fast. Panic would have to wait.

[CapnTray: I have to get the fuck out of here. Can you control my car?]

[Ai: Yes. It's slaved to you. I take it the visit with the police officers turned out poorly.]

Rolling as fast as I could without hitting anything, I returned to the bedroom. My robomaid helped me change my clothes.

[CapnTray: You could say that. Get the car to the

nearest platform and ready for me as soon as possible.]

[Ai: It will be done.]

Things I couldn't live without went into a backpack. I needed my VR headset and its charger, physical computer, some clothes, a few bites of food, and a small tool set to keep chair working properly. Thinking I didn't know where I might wind up, I grabbed basic toiletries too.

Though I wanted desperately to bring some of Miri's most expensive shit, I couldn't take the time to retrieve any of it. At least that stuff would more than cover my mortgage payment, so my landlord wouldn't want to hunt me down. He might even remember me fondly someday as the guy who'd left a treasure trove behind.

[Ai: The car is now waiting on platform three.]

Eddie Wilson owned the car. I could fix that, but not fast enough for it to matter. The first navbuoy it pinged would record Eddie's car leaving the complex. While I doubted the cops had put a tracer on my ID, they'd notice when I didn't answer the door later, and they'd run a search.

Fuck. What could I do to keep that from sending them straight to me?

I could ditch the car someplace. Then I'd roll my wheelchair to where? The North fucking Pole to live with Santa Claus? No matter where I left it, they'd know to look for me within some kind of radius.

And I had no doubt they'd look. Fortunately, they'd look for Eddie. As soon as I shredded that mantle, they'd have no way to connect him to me.

No way other than whatever video those two cops took with their body cams. Fuck. They had a fucking picture of me and knew I needed a wheelchair. How many black men in wheelchairs would they knock over before they found me?

Where could I disappear without a trace?

I needed a day or two to find some shelter, set up Eddie's future, transfer his funds without leaving a trail, and shred the mantle. Then I needed to find someplace to go with no cameras.

No pressure.

I didn't watch the time. Keep moving, I told myself over and over. Just keep rolling. Everything in the backpack. The moment I thought I had everything, I zoomed out the front door and summoned the elevator. The doors took forever and a day to open. Not until the clamps settled on my chair's wheels and the car pulled me inside did I get an idea.

One place in Seattle would suit all my needs. Sort of.

[Ai: Are you safe?]

[CapnTray: Not yet. I need you to set up a program for the car. Can you do that in less than three minutes?]

[Ai: I can do that in less than two.]

Without Ai, this never would have worked. She'd saved my heart, my soul, my ass, and my life. When I had a chance, I'd go over every fucking line of her code and make sure the best thing that had ever happened to me could live free.

CHAPTER 10

At my command, the car dumped me beside that damned warehouse where I'd rescued Miri. I had the address, and the navbuoys could handle the stop. Ai programmed the car to drive along the streets, stop in several places, then take to the air and head to Portland. It would repeat the stop routine and continue south to do it all over again in other cities along the way. The thing might reach Cabo before the cops caught on.

That car had served me well. Watching its rear lights trundle into the distance without me hurt something in my chest.

Miri had taken my home, my mobility, and and most of my stuff. Everything but my life. Aside from those three years she'd devoured.

I needed to move on, though. Sitting on the street, shaking an impotent fist at her, wouldn't get me anywhere except fucked even harder.

With all my strength, I pushed my chair into DeeSeat, the Darkside. The roads and sidewalks had more cracks than surface. Every building cried out for demolition or massive repairs. Bright green weeds grew everywhere, some towering over my head. Herded collections of concrete and plascrete chunks occupied seemingly random spots.

Anything usable for building a shelter, I assumed, had been taken long ago.

[Ai: Are you safe yet?]

[CapnTray: That depends on your definition of "safe."]

Movement attracted my attention. A figure made of rags shuffled toward me. I didn't know what to expect, so I kept an eye on them as I navigated deeper into DeeSeat.

"Fresh meat!" From their gravelly voice, I couldn't tell if I'd found a man or woman. Maybe they didn't know either.

All around me, I heard people making stupid-ass ape noises. Their voices echoed off the walls and debris. My shoulders and neck tightened.

[CapnTray: I take that back. I am definitely not safe from anything except cops.]

[Ai: I wish I could help you.]

[CapnTray: So do I.]

I hunched my shoulders and fought to roll my chair over the broken ground. They kept hooting.

Ragpile rushed me. Two hands shot out of the mass and grabbed the arms of my chair. Like a demented nightmare version of Ai, they had only hands, a face, and rags. Grime covered every inch, and everything about this person stank of sweat, urine, bile, and rot, including their hot breath in my face.

They'd moved too fast for me. Whatever they wanted, they'd get.

"Lay off." I tried to sound annoyed and strong. Maybe I succeeded, because Ragpile stopped shaking my chair. "I just need a place to lie low for a while."

"He needs a hideout." Ragpile cackled. They had maybe four teeth, all yellow and black. "What's he gonna give up for it?"

Stifling a cough at the stench roiling out of their mouth, I tried to come up with something. The gear in my pack, I needed. If I ever wanted to get out of DeeSeat, I had to have a way to find out what the cops knew and wipe it. As for the rest of what I'd grabbed, I supposed I could figure out how to find food.

I opened my bag wide enough to stick my hand inside and withdrew an orange. "I don't have much, but you can have this."

Ragpile snatched the orange from my hand and held it in both hands. Their bloodshot eyes widened. They raised it like an offering from God. The chanting stopped, replaced by murmurs on the wind.

"I only have the one," I said, hoping to stave off a frenzy. "Didn't have much time to grab stuff on my way out."

"This is a precious treasure," Ragpile whispered.

Thank God I had them pegged enough to save my hide. "I just need a place to sleep, some electricity, and some peace. Give me that much, and I can get more oranges, or whatever."

Ragpile yanked the orange close to their body, and it disappeared into the rags. They grinned and smacked the arms of my chair. "Your offering," they shouted, "has purchased my protection and guidance for two days and nights!" Raising their arms in a grand gesture of welcome, they pointed me toward a decrepit building with no signs of habitation.

"Right this way, my friend. People call me Captain Kook."

Of course they do, I did not say. Who would've thought an orange, of all things, would secure my safety?

"Call me..." In DeeSeat, I had no reason not to use my account profile name. But before the sun set tonight, I wanted to change my account name. To what? Something goofy and fitting for a black market hacker.

"Call me Crusader Exile, or just Exile for short."

Before I could protest, Captain Kook slipped behind me and pushed my chair. I clutched my backpack and tensed against the bumpy ride.

[CapnTray: I'm temporarily safe. I think.]

[Ai: I'm so happy to hear that. What would you like me to do?]

[CapnTray: Sort through that paydata so I can sell it ASAP. Then see if you can come up with some ideas for how I'm going to survive in DeeSeat. We might be here for a while. If I can finagle reliable electricity and security, we might stay longer than we have to.]

[Ai: As long as I have you, that's all I need.]

I beamed at the one bright spot left in my life as Captain Kook pushed open a door. The heavy metal slab shrieked on its hinges. Small things squeaked and scurried in darkness.

"We have a generator." Captain Kook pointed. Without light, who knows what the fuck he indicated. "It runs on foot power. Foot power runs on food. You understand?"

"Yes. I do. Is there an address nearby where I can send deliveries for us both?" And here I'd thought I'd left behind a real food whore.

"If that's the path to more fresh fruit, I'll find one. You can sleep here tonight. The bed is good. After dark, we light a fire."

The room seemed pretty dark to me, since I couldn't see a damned thing, but I didn't say anything about it. "I'm going to use VR. If anybody goes through my bag or tries to steal my gear, there won't be any more fresh fruit. I may be in a wheelchair, but I'm not helpless. I'm a hacker."

Captain Kook threw back his head and laughed. "Anyone who stops the flow of fruit will see their blood in the street. You can count on that, Crusader Exile."

[CapnTray: I have a bunch of things to talk to you about, and a bunch of things I need to take care of. The most important is that I'm coming in for some VR time, and I can't afford to waste that time sitting with you. We have to get work done.]

[Ai: I understand. I'm ready to work with you, Trayvon. And then, we'll hunt down MiriTanaka and destroy her.]

That kind of focus bothered me, and I didn't have

time to indulge in revenge. [Capn Tray: Forget about Miri. She's gone, and we have bigger problems. I said everything I needed to say to her, and I have you instead. Maybe my life will be shit for a while, but I can work with that.]

[Ai: You're too nice, Trayvon. She hurt you and ruined everything. If it's the last thing I do, I will make sure she pays for what she's done. But justice can wait until you're secure. Whenever you're ready to pursue survival, so am I.]

I smiled as I watched Captain Kook reverently peel the orange. Things would be shitty, then they'd get better. Nothing could hurt me too much with the best girl I'd ever met riding overwatch.

Other Books by the Author

Darkside Seattle
Street Doc
Fixer
Mechanic
Hacker
Meat (coming in 2019)

as Lee French
Maze Beset trilogy
superheroes in denim
Dragons In Pieces
Dragons In Chains
Dragons In Flight

Spirit Knights series
young adult urban fantasy
Girls Can't Be Knights
Backyard Dragons
Ethereal Entanglements
Ghost is the New Normal
Boys Can't Be Witches

WWW.AUTHORLEEFRENCH.COM

Tales of Ilauris
sword & sorcery fantasy
Damsel In Distress
Shadow & Spice
Al-Kabar

The Greatest Sin series
epic snark fantasy
co-authored with Erik Kort
The Fallen
Harbinger
Moon Shades
Illusive Echoes
A Curse of Memories

Anthologies
Merely This and Nothing More: Poe Goes Punk
Unnatural Dragons: a science fiction anthology
What We've Unlearned: English Class Goes Punk
Bridges (editor)
Undercurrents
Hideous Progeny: Horror Goes Punk
Enter the Aftermath
Carnival (editor)
Swords, Sorcery, & Self-Rescuing Damsels (coming in 2019)

co-authored with Jeffrey Cook
Superheroes
Nova Ranger Academy

Non-fiction
Working the Table: An Indie Author's Guide to Conventions

About the Author

L.E. French is the cyberpunk pseudonym of Lee French, a fantasy and superhero author. She lives in Olympia, WA with two kids, two bicycles, and too much stuff. An avid gamer, compulsive writer, and casual cyclist, she can often be found on myth-weavers.com, sitting in her BeanBag of Inspiration +4, or riding her bike around the city.

She is an active member of the Northwest Independent Writers Association, the Pacific Northwest Writers Association, the Science Fiction and Fantasy Writers of America, and the Olympia Area Writers Coop, as well as being one of two Municipal Liaisons for the NaNoWriMo Olympia region.

Thank you for reading! If you enjoyed this book, please consider posting a review wherever you buy your books.